BEYOND GLORY

ANNE SCHRAFF

STANDING TALL MYSTERIES
BY ANNE SCHRAFF

Project Editor: Carol E. Newell
Cover Designer and Illustrator: TSA design group

© 1995 Saddleback Publishing, Inc.

SADDLEBACK
PUBLISHING • INC.

3505 Cadillac Ave., Building F-9
Costa Mesa, CA 92626

ISBN 1-56254-151-X
Printed in the United States of America
03 02 01 M 99 98 97 96   8 7 6 5 4 3 2 1

Chapter 1

Whenever Micah Newton passed the trophy case at Wilson High, an electric charge of pride went through him. He was back in the stadium again for the big county-wide championship game— the Wilson Wildcats against their bitter rivals, the Garfield Fireballs. Micah was the quarterback for the Wildcats. When he carried the ball all the way into the end zone for the winning touchdown the roar of the crowd was awesome.

Once more a grin broke Micah's face as he entered Wilson's front doors, but the grin soon faded. Coach Tommie Benson and Floyd Anders, the janitor, stood at the shattered trophy case and walls sprayed with graffiti. The graffiti carried a simple message—*football stinks.*

"What happened?" Micah asked, shoving his way to the front of the crowd of students.

Coach Benson shook his head sadly. "Somebody busted in here last night and stole the championship trophy and trashed just about everything else," he said. "All the athletic plaques are spray painted ..."

Anders swept the shards of glass into a dust pan. "Stop the world—I wanna get off. What are they gonna do next?" he muttered.

The hurt spread through Micah like a fever. Some creep had spoiled that golden day of glory for him when the crowd chanted and the cheerleaders twirled in a spinning riot of blue and gold.

"The police are checking it out," Coach Benson said, "but they've got a lot of *serious* crime to worry about ..."

Jason Hawley came walking up. He

stood on the sidelines for a few minutes without saying a word. He used to be star quarterback for the Wildcats. It seemed he couldn't do anything wrong. And then, suddenly, he couldn't do anything right. He fumbled, he missed passes. The cheers turned to boos. Coach Benson replaced him with Micah and the Wildcats hadn't lost a game since. Jason never said much, but the pain in his eyes told the whole story. He was heartbroken about being side-lined.

When Micah met Jason's gaze, Jason said, "Too bad." He said it without much feeling.

"I wonder who did it," Micah said. "Somebody with a grudge, huh?"

"Maybe guys from Garfield," Jason said. "They were pretty ticked off when they lost the championship."

Micah watched Jason walk away. He didn't want to suspect Jason—Jason was a friend. But Jason had a tough sports-minded father who drove his son hard. Jason had good cause to be bitter about football.

The janitor continued to sweep and Micah helped him empty the glass into trash bags. Anders was a big shouldered man, his once black hair frosted with silver. "Did you ever play football, Mr. Anders?" Micah asked.

Anders smiled. "Ahh, don't call me Mister Anders, boy. I'm Floyd—good old Floyd. And, yeah, I played football. I was an offensive lineman."

Micah nodded. "I bet you were good. You're big."

"Uh huh. I played for the Wildcats. You can see me in the old yearbooks if they've got any left from the old days when I was young," Anders laughed.

"Oh, you're not *that* old, Floyd," Micah said.

"Well, let's put it this way. When Abe Lincoln traveled by train, I used to wave to him!" Anders said.

Micah headed for his first class. He pulled his history book from his locker and, as he did, a note tumbled out. The note was a paste-up job made of cut up magazines. Written across a newspaper account of one of Micah's top games were the words *ha ha ha ha ha*. Micah was stunned. Could the vandalism have been directed against him personally?

Chapter 2

Micah slid into his desk in history a few minutes before class. Kaitlin West, his girlfriend, looked up. "I saw what they did to the trophy case, Micah. That was so low. I'm sorry, Micah. I know how much pride you took in the championship trophy."

Micah showed Kaitlin the note he found in his locker. "I think maybe whoever did it was trying to hurt *me*."

"Oh, how stupid! How mean and stupid. But who'd do that? Hey, Micah, remember that big, tough quarterback with the Fireballs from Garfield—Beau Shaw? Remember him? He looked like he could bite the heads off nails when you beat him. I bet he did it," Kaitlin said.

"But how would a guy from Garfield get into my history book? Had to be somebody I sat near in class who shoved it in when I wasn't looking," Micah said.

"Beau probably has a girlfriend at Wilson," Kaitlin said.

"Well, it sure was a dirty trick to steal our trophy. All the guys on the team worked hard to win that season," Micah said.

Jason came into class and went to his seat in the back. As he did, Kaitlin leaned over to Micah and whispered, "Maybe he did it. His father was so mad when he got sidelined that he made Jason run punishment laps all around the neighborhood. Jason almost dropped from exhaustion, but there stood Mr. Hawley yelling, 'Five more laps, stupid. Maybe that will teach you not to fumble footballs'."

"Man, I didn't know that," Micah

said.

Jason didn't show up for football practice after school. "Hawley's off the team if he skips another practice," Coach Benson snapped.

"Maybe he's feeling bad about the football stuff getting vandalized," a boy said. Laughter greeted the remark.

Another lineman said, "Hawley probably did the vandalism himself! Ever since he got pushed out of the limelight he's been a sour pickle."

Floyd Anders walked by just then, picking trash off the playing field. "Hey Floyd, got all the johns cleaned already?" a boy shouted.

"Yep," Anders shouted back. He didn't seem to mind the teasing.

"You're the best janitor in the district, man," another boy laughed, "they oughta give you a trophy."

"Like a golden john," another boy roared.

"Be sure and spell my name right

when you engrave it," Anders said.

"Knock it off, you guys," Coach Benson snapped. "Stop hassling Floyd."

"Aw, he don't mind, Coach," a kicker said. His name was Luther. He led the pack in making fun of Floyd. But he didn't mean anything by it.

"No grown man likes that kind of stuff," Benson growled. "Let's practice football, okay?"

The practice went well and when the team returned to the locker room everybody was in good spirits.

"Hey!" Micah shouted, "somebody slashed my jacket!"

"Mine, too," Luther cried. "Oh, man!"

Coach Benson came over. "This is awful! I can't ever remember a thing like this happening. Somebody must've come in while we practiced...."

"Coach," Luther yelled, "there's Jason Hawley skulking around. How come he didn't come to practice?"

Coach Benson, Micah, and Luther went outside and called to Jason. He ignored them, jogging towards his pickup truck.

"He's guilty as sin," Luther snarled. "Look at him go!"

"Hold on," Coach Benson said, "we aren't sure of anything yet."

Micah hurried towards his motorcycle in the parking lot. He intended to follow Jason and get some answers himself. He loved his football jacket and it cost a lot of money. Nobody was getting away with trashing it!

Chapter 3

Micah caught up to Jason at a light. "Hey, man," Micah yelled, "pull over. We've got to talk."

Jason pulled over and got out, walking back to Micah. "What's up?" he asked.

"How come you didn't stop when the Coach was yelling at you?" Micah asked.

An angry look crossed Jason's face. "I don't need Benson on my back about missing practice. I get enough hassle at home," he said.

"Jason, somebody went in the locker room and slashed my jacket and Luther's jacket. We figured it happened while we were at practice," Micah said.

"Oh ... I get it," Jason said, his eyes narrowing, "you think I did it. That's what you think, don't you? Come on, man, say it out loud. Stop jiving around."

"I'm not accusing anybody," Micah said.

"You don't need to. It's all over your face. Why would I do it, man?" Jason asked.

"Some of the guys think you got a grudge against the team," Micah said.

"Me? Just 'cause Benson sidelined me for a couple of bad plays? Just 'cause he's probably wrecked my chances of looking good when college scouts come around and offer scholarships?" Jason said.

"I hear the bitterness in your voice, Jason," Micah said softly, "and I can understand it."

"Don't talk to me in that pitying tone, man. I don't need that. My father thinks the only way out of this neighborhood is through football, but there are other ways," Jason said.

"Sure," Micah agreed, "like making good grades and learning skills."

Jason laughed harshly. "Stuff that kind of talk in the john, man."

"Look, Jason—," Micah began, but Jason turned sharply and walked back to his pickup. He looked back once.

"Yes, I hate that football trophy and I don't care if your football jackets got trashed, but I didn't do it, okay? I got bigger fish to fry!" With that he jumped back in his truck and roared off.

Micah returned to the locker room, far from sure of Jason's guilt or innocence.

"Did he admit it?" Luther demanded.

"No, he denied it," Micah said.

"Yeah, right!" Luther said. "With me sitting on his back and pounding his face into the pavement maybe he'll admit it!"

"Put a lid on that kind of talk," Coach Benson said. "Any rough stuff and you're off the team."

Micah examined his damaged jacket sadly. It could be repaired, but it would never look the same. He'd been so proud of it. Both Micah's parents worked, but with four kids in the family there was no money for a new jacket.

As Micah rode his motorcycle home, a car slowed alongside him. It was filled with guys from Garfield. "Hey, Newton, heard about your trophy getting ripped off," Beau Shaw shouted. "What a shame!" The whole car rocked with laughter and jeering. Micah tried to ignore it but they continued to ride alongside him, taunting him.

"Next Friday, the Lincoln Lancers are gonna soften you up," Beau yelled, "and the next Friday after that the Fireballs are going to burn your tails."

"Prove it on the field, man," Micah

yelled.

"We're going to sack you so many times you're going to feel like a pound of potatoes, Newton!" a lineman laughed.

"Say it with points on the scoreboard, not with talking trash, man," Micah said.

Micah turned into his driveway and, as he did, an overripe tomato smashed into the back of his already ripped jacket. Boiling with rage, Micah leaped off the motorcycle, his hands tightening into fists.

Chapter 4

To Micah's surprise, the tomato didn't come from the car full of Fireballs. A kid of about twelve hurled it.

"You little punk," Micah yelled, taking off down the street after the tall, thin boy.

"You catch me when you catch the moon, you big fool," the boy screamed.

"Wanna bet?" Micah shouted, gaining on the boy and grabbing his shirttail, bringing him up short.

"Lemme go," the boy screamed, squirming and kicking at Micah.

"Hey," Micah said, "you're Floyd Anders' kid, Junior."

"So what?" Junior aimed a kick at Micah's shins, but Micah dodged it.

"Floyd's a good guy. What would he say about you throwing rotten tomatoes at people like that?" Micah demanded.

"I don't care what he says. He's got no time, and I got no time for him," Junior said.

"He once played football," Micah said, trying to reach the boy. "Didn't you know that?"

"That's old stuff. Anyway, I don't believe it. He's just a dirty old dustman. Who cares about him?" Junior sneered.

"Look, don't you be throwing fruit at people, boy—or somebody is going to whip you good," Micah declared.

Junior looked at him with sullen eyes. Micah finally released him and he darted away yelling, "I hope the Lincoln Lancers stomp all over your head!"

Micah went inside his house to find his father making pizza. His parents were both restaurant cooks, and they took turns cooking for the family.

"Dad, that Anders boy is a mean one," Micah said. "What's his problem?"

"His mom is gone and his father drinks," Dad answered.

"Floyd Anders is such a nice, easy-going guy at school," Micah said. "Everybody likes him."

"Like you'd like a dog," Dad said. "But a man wants more respect."

Micah felt very weary. "It's been a bad day, Dad. Real bad. Somebody stole the championship trophy. And then me and Luther got our jackets ripped. Looks like somebody hates the football team or something."

"What a cheap shot to take," Dad said. He crimped the edges of the pizza dough and poured on the sauce.

"Oh, Dad, I almost forgot. I got an A in Physics," Micah said.

Dad came over, a big grin spreading on his face. He slapped Micah on the back so hard he almost knocked his son over. "By golly! An A in Physics! Where do you get those smarts, boy? An A in Physics!"

Micah stared at his father. He didn't act that way when Micah helped the Wildcats win the championship!

"It's only an A on a test, Dad," Micah said.

"Micah, someday you'll be doing an important job using the principles of physics. Maybe you'll be designing a road or helping to build a big complex. That's really something."

"Dad, football is important, too," Micah said. "I could get a football scholarship, and then you guys wouldn't have to worry about getting money for me to go to college."

"Micah, you're going to college. Maybe your Mom and I will have to beg or borrow the money. Maybe the both of us will have to work two jobs each, but with or without a football scholarship, *you are going to college.* I swear to that, son," Dad said, his voice shaking with emotion.

Micah got up and gave his father a hug. "It's just that losing that championship trophy has really got me down, Dad."

"Keep your mind on physics, Micah, and on history and English. Football is phony glory, boy, but what you learn in school ... that's beyond glory."

Chapter 5

The stands were packed for the game between the Wilson Wildcats and the Lincoln Lancers. Micah was more tense than he usually was before a game. The vandalism had rattled him. The Lancers were not a very good team but Micah had to fight against blowing off the challenge and thinking about next week's game against the Fireballs.

"This is going to be a piece of cake," Luther said confidently before the kick-off.

"Don't be too sure," Micah warned. "The Lancers have been spoilers before for teams like ours."

"Yeah," Jason said, "they can sneak up on you and once they get possession, they score." Jason looked right at Micah. "You look scared, man. It was like that the night I started fumbling...."

Micah thought Jason was deliberately trying to spook him. After all, if Micah fouled up, then Coach Benson might give Jason another chance at quarterback. "You looking to jinx me, Jason?" Micah asked.

Jason sort of sneered. "I can feel what's going to happen. The Lancers are going to get the ball and the points are going to start piling up, and you'll start to sweat, and that'll only make it worse. You'll fumble the ball and they'll get it ... yeah, they can smell fear, man, and you got fear in your eyes."

"Hey," Coach Benson yelled, "what are you gabbing about Hawley? Leave Newton alone to get his mind on the plays."

Jason winked at Micah and whispered, "You're going to remember this night all your life 'cause they'll wipe the field up with your jersey."

The teams ran out on the field to the cheers of their fans. It was a Wilson home game so there were more Wilson fans. They made more noise, but the Lincoln fans tried to make up for it by really screaming.

Micah saw Kaitlin leading the Wilson cheerleaders, leaping and dancing in a new cheer she learned at camp. Micah saw his father in the stands, too, but he was reading the newspaper. Jason's dad was there, too. He was a big, muscular, mean-looking guy with arms like the trunks of oak trees. No wonder Jason obeyed him and ran all those punishment laps, Micah thought.

With his first possession of the ball, Micah looked for an opening and passed to Jason. The Lancers crowded Jason, but Jason sprinted free and galloped right into the end zone for the first touchdown of the game. The stands exploded in cheers. Jason's dad was jumping up and down and screaming his lungs out.

Then the Lancers made a touchdown and the score was tied. Micah fumbled the ball and the Lancers recovered, but the Wildcats defense forced another turnover. Once more Jason got the ball and ran with it for his second touchdown. Jason was dazzling, and Micah was flat. At half time, Coach Benson said, "Play like that all the time, Hawley, and you'll get your position back! What's your problem, Newton? Didn't you get enough sleep last night?"

Micah exploded into action for the second half, getting back-to-back touchdowns. "New-ton, New-ton!" came the chanting from the stands. Jason got rattled and couldn't seem to do anything right. The Wildcats permanently went ahead to win the game with the fans screaming "Micah, the man! Micah, the main man!"

After the game, as Micah headed for home, he saw Jason with his father. "So, what went wrong, fool?" his father demanded.

"I don't know, Dad!" Jason snapped.

"I'm asking you a question, fool," Jason's father said, blocking the boy from getting in the car.

"I don't know," Jason said.

Micah heard a sharp slap. When he looked again Jason's head hung low and he was rubbing his smarting face. Micah felt sick.

Chapter 6

"Great game, son," Micah's father said when Micah got in the car.

"Thanks, Dad," Micah said, trying to forget the horrible scene he had just seen between Jason and his dad.

"Know what, Micah? I read this magazine article that said knowing physics opens up all kinds of careers in chemistry, and astronomy. That's exciting!" Dad said.

"Did you see my last touchdown, Dad? Was that amazing or what?" Micah asked.

"Yeah, that was swell," Dad said.

"Dad, don't you like football?" Micah asked.

"I love football. Don't I come to all

your games?" Dad laughed.

"You weren't good at it in school, were you, Dad?" Micah asked.

"No. I played, but I was pretty lame," Dad admitted. "What burned me up was that the prettiest girls went for the football players, but I got lucky. Your mom went for me even though she was the prettiest girl in school."

"You and Floyd Anders go to school together, Dad?" Micah asked.

"Yeah. He was a senior when I was a junior. He was the only guy in our school who won a good scholarship," Dad said. "To a Big Ten school."

"No kidding!" Micah said, gaining new respect for Floyd. "Did he ever play pro ball?"

Dad shrugged. "He helped his college win a national championship, but then he got injured ... came limping home. Pulled a tendon I guess. He told me that after playing football for so long, everything hurt, even his big toes.

Said his one big toe wouldn't even bend any more."

"Man, he's like a celebrity or something, though," Micah said, "playing for a Big Ten school and helping win a national championship. He's big time. I wonder why he isn't teaching with his college degree."

"Didn't get a degree," Dad said. "Flunked."

"Oh," Micah said.

At school on Monday, Jason walked up to Micah at the lockers. "If it hadn't been for you I woulda been the big hero at Friday's game. You put me in the shade, Newton," Jason said bitterly.

"Jason, we're supposed to be teammates, remember? We won, didn't we?" Micah said.

"You won," Jason said. "You were using every move to make me look bad."

"You're crazy. I even passed to you," Micah said. "Man, get with it!

Next Friday we have got a major game against the Fireballs. We've got to be together, as a team. They'll be out for revenge. This is the first game since we won the championship. We gotta win, Jason!"

Jason sneered in Micah's face and snarled, "Don't you get it, man? My old man wants me to look good. He wants me to be a football hero so the scouts come waving scholarships under my nose. He thinks I'm gonna play some-day for the Cowboys or the Oilers and make megabucks for him and Mom. That's where it's at, man!" Jason blocked Micah from moving.

"So go for it, Jason. I'm not stopping you," Micah snapped, shoving Jason away.

"Don't push me, man," Jason growled.

"I'm not pushing you. You're in the way. Get your hands off me. You got a head problem, man!" Micah shouted, walking away.

"Know what, Micah?" Jason declared to Micah's back. "Your girlfriend, Kaitlin, is all upset. You better go check it out in the auditorium."

Micah turned cold. If Jason did something to hurt Kaitlin ...

Chapter 7

Micah went to the auditorium where Kaitlin and several other girls were rehearsing for the school musical. Micah stood in the doorway watching Kaitlin twirl gracefully around. She was so beautiful that Micah forgot about everything in his pleasure at seeing her dance. Finally she broke from the others and came down the aisle towards him. "Hi, Micah," she said.

"Kaitlin, you looked so terrific dancing. But is everything okay? Jason was saying something about you being all upset, so I came to check.... I thought that creep did something to upset you just to mess up my mind," Micah said.

"Somebody grabbed one of Floyd's

slop buckets and threw it all over the cheerleader outfits. It's a big mess," Kaitlin said. "Some of the girls were crying ...uh ... maybe I was, too, a little."

"Jason Hawley did it," Micah cried. "He won't get away with this!"

"Oh, Micah, don't get in a big fight with him," Kaitlin said. "You'll just get suspended and that'll be playing right into his hands. I don't want you bounced from the team over dirty cheerleader outfits."

"I'm not going to fight him. I'm going to tell Coach Benson what he did. He'll get bounced from the team then, Kaitlin," Micah said. "I think Jason is the one who stole the championship trophy and slashed our jackets, too. He's not fit to play on the team."

Micah found Coach Benson at his desk and told him everything. Benson sent for Jason, pulling him from Spanish class. When Jason came in he glared at Micah. "Ratted on me, huh?" he said.

"Jason, did you throw all the cheerleader costumes in a heap and douse them with dirty water?" Benson asked.

"It was a joke, that's all," Jason said. "What's the big deal?"

"And how about slashing my jacket and Luther's jacket?" Micah demanded. "Was that a joke, too?"

"I didn't do that," Jason said grimly. "And I didn't mess with the trophy case, either."

Coach Benson shook his head. "Jason, you've got a lot of natural athletic ability. You're a fine football player. For the first part of the season you were the best quarterback I ever saw at Wilson. You could be as great as Flash Anders was when he played here twenty years ago. But you've got an attitude problem that's going to mess up your whole life if you don't get a handle on it. As things now stand, you're out of Friday's game."

.

"I'll pay to have the girls' costumes cleaned, Coach," Jason said anxiously. "You can't suspend me. My father is coming to that game ..."

"Jason," Coach Benson said, "I know you have problems at home, son. There's nothing I hate quite so much as a 'football dad', some guy who bullies his son into playing so hard that all the fun is squeezed out of the game. I can't help your dad's attitude, but you have to work on yours. I'm not going to blame you for the trophy vandalism or the damaged jackets until we have proof. If I find out you did those things, you're off the team, period. But if you pay to have the girls' outfits cleaned, then we'll see about Friday."

"Thanks, Coach," Jason said in a husky voice.

"Just watch your step, Jason," Coach Benson said. "If there's any more trouble I promise you, you will never put on a Wildcats uniform again!"

Micah watched Jason peel off some bills to pay for the cleaning job. Then Micah turned and walked back to his next class. Jason had a wild look on his face. Micah figured he'd be downright dangerous if he saw football being taken out of his life right now.

Chapter 8

Micah ate lunch with Kaitlin under a big pepper tree the next day. "Sometimes I hate football," she said.

"Hate football?" Micah laughed. "What happened to that little girl in pigtails? She used to demand to play in the games we had in the parking lot behind the hamburger stand."

"That was different," Kaitlin said. "That was fun—pure fun. All the kids playing and tumbling around and laughing and not caring who won. Then we'd go for cheeseburgers or tacos and sodas ..."

"Kaitlin, you are the head cheerleader. I see you jumping up and down and screaming at the games. You're the most spirited cheerleader on the squad in that cute little blue and gold pleated skirt. Who are you telling you hate football?" Micah asked.

"Oh, Micah, I'm cheering *you*, and I'm cheering for the guys, but it gets so nasty. I mean cars full of kids from the other side cursing us and throwing stuff. A guy killed another fan with a baseball bat at a high school game! And when guys get hurt and have to be carried off, some of the fans cheer like they're glad somebody has to go to the hospital. It's just so nasty ..." Kaitlin said, her voice trailing off.

"You're just upset over Jason acting like he did," Micah said.

"I feel sorry for him, Micah," Kaitlin said.

"Sorry for him when he spilled slimy water all over your outfits?" Micah asked.

"You don't live across the street from him, Micah. You don't see that dad of his making his life miserable. I've seen him make Jason take a toothbrush and clean out every garbage pail in the alley just for fumbling at a game. And all the younger kids watch and laugh at Jason, like that mean little Anders kid, Junior. I'm telling you, it makes me sick," Kaitlin said.

"Jason oughn't let his dad bully him like that," Micah said.

"Oh, Micah, he'll whip Jason when he's good and mad. Jason's mom just stands there and cries," Kaitlin said.

Micah took a deep breath and finished his sandwich. Sure, Jason had a mean dad. That was too bad. But that didn't give him the right to trash the trophy case or rip up jackets, if he was the one who did it.

As Micah passed the small room where Floyd Anders kept his cleaning supplies he stopped. "Hey, Floyd, my Dad told me you played for a Big Ten school. I never knew that."

Floyd nodded. "I admit to the crime."

"Which school?" Micah asked. "I bet it was Michigan."

"Ahh, that's all ancient history. It was back when dinosaurs roamed the earth, boy," the janitor said.

"Hey, don't blow it off, Floyd. It's something to be proud of," Micah said.

Anders turned, mop in hand, "Proud of? How so?"

"Well, like that's what we're all shooting for, a college scholarship, playing for a school that's a football power. Then maybe pro ball. It must have been exciting, Floyd. You got to play in a bowl game, huh?"

"Yep, we played in the soup bowl. We threw spoons at each other," Anders joked.

"You ... uh ... don't like to reminisce, huh Floyd?" Micah asked.

"What's done is done and can't be undone. I believe somebody important said that. The past is dead and buried. Who wants to dig up bones?"

Micah was shocked to see the deep sadness in the man's weary eyes. Floyd Anders seemed almost near tears.

Chapter 9

Luther came along and Micah walked with him to class. "Floyd sure doesn't like to talk about the old glory days, Luther," Micah said.

"Yeah. You know, he played in two Rose Bowl games. I looked it up. He was a big star. Picture in the papers and stuff. Our old yearbooks are full of him, too," Luther said.

"Man," Micah said, "if that ever happened to me I'd have scrapbooks and bore everybody with football stories. I'd probably have movies of all my games, and I'd play them over and over."

Luther laughed. "I saw a movie once where the guy did that all the time."

"What kind of job did the guy in the movie have?" Micah asked.

Luther scratched his head, trying to remember. "I don't think he had a job … I think he just … uh … watched his old football movies."

Jason seemed very quiet over the next few days. Micah hoped he was going to try to get his act together. Micah hated to see him so down, almost as if he'd lost his spirit. Coach Benson hadn't yet decided about letting Jason play Friday. Micah decided he'd try to put in a good word for him, for old times sake.

"Coach," Micah said, "I've been thinking. I'm still not sure if Jason had anything to do with that vandalism of the trophy case, but we learned in Civics that a guy is innocent until proven guilty."

"What are you driving at, Micah?" Benson asked.

"Well ... uh ... he did pay for getting the girls' outfits cleaned up, right?" Micah asked.

"Yes, he did. I think it'd maybe be good if he got the chance to play on Friday. It means an awful lot to him. What do you think, Micah?" Benson asked.

"Yeah," Micah said with a grin. "I'm thinking the same thing, Coach. I mean, I don't want to tell you your business and stuff. Jason is really feeling down. If he could play I think he'd try harder to shape up."

Coach Benson nodded and winked. "Well, I'll certainly give it serious consideration, Micah."

Jason suited up for practice on Wednesday. He avoided Micah and dutifully practiced every play like an eager kid trying out for a team. Micah wasn't sure how to read it. Was Jason really guilty of all the vandalism and was he trying to be so good that he wouldn't be suspected anymore? Or was he innocent and anxious to prove his worth?

Micah tried not to think about Jason as he prepared for the game. The Fireballs had a bad reputation for fouling other players. Several of their games last season ended in fights that spilled over into the stands. The Fireballs were eager for revenge after losing the championship last year and that would make them twice as tough.

"This may be the biggest game I've ever been in, Mom," Micah said the night before. "I mean, the newspaper guys will be there. It's a revenge match between the Wildcats and the Fireballs."

Mom paused in stirring her cheese sauce. "You make it sound like a war, honey."

"Well, it sort of is. I mean this might be my big chance to shine and get the eye of a college scout," Micah said.

"Baby," Mom said, "you shine every day. Every time you make a good grade, every time you make a friend, every time you do us proud ..."

"Thanks, Mom," Micah said, glad his parents weren't like Jason's dad. But still it was *important* to win that big game and look good doing it. *It was!*

Chapter 10

The game was at Garfield and in spite of two bus loads of Wilson fans and a lot of cars, the Wilson boosters were outnumbered. *You're in Fireball Country!*, proclaimed a huge banner as they entered the school. Micah caught the eye of a grinning Beau Shaw. "You're gonna get fried, man," Shaw shouted. "It's pay back time."

The Fireballs raced onto the playing field in their scarlet jerseys like meteors. Then came the Wildcats in their blue and gold. It was kickoff time and within a few seconds the Fireballs had scored. Thunder from the stands rocked the field. Micah quickly got possession of the ball and, as he was looking to pass, a huge Fireball crashed into him, driving him down to the dirt. It was a foul and the Fireballs were penalized, but Micah was hurt. He could barely get back to the bench under his own power.

Coach Benson had no choice but to bring in Jason as quarterback. Jason Hawley was hot and had made two touchdowns by half time. Micah watched it all with mixed feelings. It was going to be a great night for his team, but it was all Jason. It was Jason's glory, not his. Jason sprinted to his third touchdown in the second half, leaving the bewildered defensive linemen from Garfield in his wake.

After the game Micah walked over to Jason. "You were awesome, man," he said.

"Thanks. Hey, you okay?" Jason asked.

"Yeah, just a little sore," Micah replied.

When Micah and Kaitlin were heading home, a ripe tomato hit the side of their car. "That Anders kid," Micah snapped. "It must've made him mad that Wilson won!" Micah got out of the car and followed the boy as he zigzagged home. Even though Micah had sore ribs, he wasn't going to let Junior get away with this.

Junior raced into the front door of his house and tried to slam it, but Micah stuck a foot in, blocking the door. Then, just beyond the door, Micah saw him. Floyd Anders was half asleep in a chair in front of the television, beer bottles littered around him.

Micah came in slowly. "Mr. Anders? Floyd?" he whispered.

Anders got up. "Whaddaya want?" he mumbled.

"Uh ... your son ... he," Micah began, then stopped. He saw the championship football trophy that had been stolen from Wilson High School. He was using it as a doorstop.

"Yeah," Anders said in a slurred voice. "I took it. You want it? Take it back. I don't care. I slashed your stupid jackets, too ... I wore one like them, once. I figured football was everything. Yeah, ha! I went to college. But I never got no education. Just played football. Thas' all they wanted me for, football. Thas' no golden dream. Thas' a lie, boy. A dirty, rotten lie ..."

Micah picked up the trophy and blew the dust off of it. He glanced at Junior who was hanging his head in deep, angry shame. Then Micah walked back to the car where Kaitlin waited.

"Here's the trophy," Micah said slowly. "Turned out Floyd found it in a trash can. He was going to return it tomorrow."

Kaitlin leaned over and kissed Micah's cheek. "Let's get cheeseburgers and sodas," she said. "Let's just have some fun again."